Steve Weatherill live of
South Lincolnshire w.s,
Luke and Tom, and th y and Sir
Gandard.

He has written and illustrated many books for children,
including *The Very First Lucy Goose Book*, *Lucy Goose
and Friends*, *Lucy's Year* and *The Crazy Christmas Puzzle
Book*. He is now working on an animated television series
about Lucy Goose.

This Young Piper first published 1991 by Pan Books Ltd,
Cavaye Place, London SW10 9PG

3 5 7 9 8 6 4 2

Text and illustrations © Steve Weatherill 1991
The right of Steve Weatherill to be
identified as author of this work
has been asserted by him in
accordance with the Copyright,
Designs and Patents Act 1988.

ISBN 0 330 31642 7

Photoset by Parker Typesetting Service, Leicester
Printed and bound in Great Britain by
Clays Ltd, St Ives plc

Look Out, It's Lucy Goose!

Steve Weatherill

Contents

It was early morning in Fen End and Lucy Goose was very excited. The postman had just been and left her lots and lots of letters.

At the very bottom of the pile was a small, square envelope.

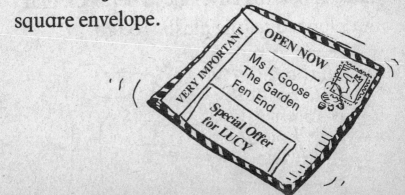

Inside the envelope was a letter. It seemed to be addressed to someone else, but she read it anyway.

Dear Ms Moose,
   You have been chosen from all the anysmels in Hen Bend to take part in our **WORLD FAMOUS SINGING COMPETITION**. Top Prizes For **ALL** The WINNERS. **AS SEEN ON T.V.**
 All you have to do is send for our course of 500 singing lessons.
To get you started, here is Lesson One and Two, COMPLETELY FREE and without obligation.

Yours in tune,
Henry Caruso
(Junior)

I've been chosen to take part in a **singing competition**... and I've got two free lessons!

Lucy shook the envelope in her beak and out plopped a little plastic record.

What a nice man. I'll go and put it on the record player right away.

With her feet slightly apart and her toes tightly gripping the grass, Lucy took a deep breath.

Godfrey Gander and Dick Duck were having a quiet drink . . . SUDDENLY!

Deep down in his front hole, Noel Vole was busy polishing his burrowing trophies.

Betty Bantam was just in the middle of
laying an egg . . .

The goslings were having a nap behind
the straw stack . . .

The frog was dozing on his rock . . .

Lucy practised the first lesson
ALL DAY and ALL NIGHT!

The other animals in Fen End just couldn't get to sleep. Lucy's singing was so loud that it could be heard all over the countryside. So early next morning, feeling very tired and very grumpy, they held a meeting.

The animals were still arguing and complaining when two strangers came strolling towards them. They were small and thin with long bodies and short stumpy legs. They wore the sort of smiles only seen in toothpaste ads. Each one carried a large suitcase.

Rob opened his suitcase and pulled out a pair of plastic headphones.

These 'ere earphones work like magic. Just put them on and you will hear nothing except your favourite sleepy time tunes... thousands of satisfied customers, your sleep is guaranteed... Will fit any size head, any size ears. For just a teeny weeny down payment... Nothing more to pay until February. Then easily-weasely payments once a week and...

A sweet lullaby will gently waft you to the land of Nod.

Suddenly, the We-Sell talk was completely drowned out by an incredibly loud

DOH!

Quick! I'll have one. She's started again.

And me!

Me too!

In a flash, every animal was wearing a
pair of magic headphones. Now
all they could hear was sweet soothing
music.

'We'll take them,' they said
in sign language.

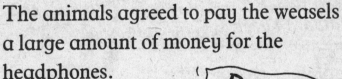

The animals agreed to pay the weasels
a large amount of money for the
headphones.

Noel Vole was so pleased that he invited the weasels to his hole for a cup of tea.

Noel was delighted with the weasels'
interest in his trophies. Rob was
especially interested in how much they
weighed. Del was interested in how many
were made of pure gold and solid silver.

That night, all the animals made sure
that they got a good night's sleep.
Each one was wearing a
pair of magic headphones.

Long before midnight they were all
sound asleep. Even Lucy, who was tired
out after another day's non-stop
singing lesson. Everybody in Fen End
was asleep, except for two . . .

Yes, you guessed.
Del and Rob, the
weasels, were up.
And they were up
to no good.

Hiss... No need to
tiptoe, Del. They
can't hear a thing
with those
headphones
on.

First the weasels went to Godfrey's nest
and stole his scooter.

Just what we
need for a quick
get-a-way, Rob.

Then they rode over to Betty Bantam's
house and stole her egg basket.

Their last stop was Noel Vole's hole and
his collection of gold and silver
burrowing trophies.

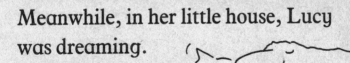

Meanwhile, in her little house, Lucy
was dreaming.

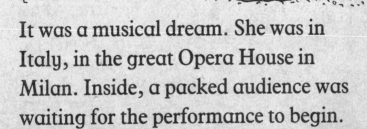

It was a musical dream. She was in
Italy, in the great Opera House in
Milan. Inside, a packed audience was
waiting for the performance to begin.

Then someone sitting in the front row
whispers, 'She's coming.'
Yes, here she comes.
That legendary opera singer.
That world-famous prima donna.
That towering titan of the tonsils . . .

LA GANSA!

Into the spotlight steps Lucy. Wrapped around her neck is a string of pearls the size of bantam's eggs.

She bows.
A low murmur runs through the theatre.
She takes a deep breath.
You could have heard a flea sneeze.
She opens her beak.
A postman in the front row faints.

Then she sings.

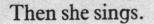

> DOH–RAY–ME–FAR–SO–LA–TI–DOH!

There is uproar.
People jump to their feet.

They shower her with flowers and
cabbages until she can't eat any more . . .
The dream made Lucy so excited that she
woke up.

Lucy dashed over to the record-player and turned over the record. She turned up the volume as far as it would go. Then she ran out and jumped in the bath.

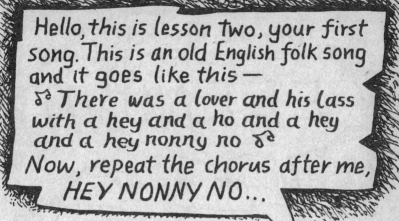

Just then, the needle jumped. There was a deep scratch on the record.

Lucy sang at the top of her voice.

Meanwhile, deep down in Noel Vole's hole, the two weasels were busy loading gold and silver trophies into Betty Bantam's basket.

EEEENONNEENONN

But they still heard the shrill sound of Lucy's singing. It sounded to them like the noise they were most afraid of.

What's that noise, Rob?

Oh, it's er... probably a burglar alarm or a night patrol goose...

BURGLAR ALARM? PATROL GOOSE? HELP! I'm getting out of here!

Rob dropped the vase he was holding and ran for the door. 'Wait for me!' yelled Del.

Two other animals were not wearing headphones in Fen End that night. They were Bill and Bob, the night patrol geese. They were patrolling the Big Pond when they heard Lucy's singing.

NON EEE NONN EEE NONN

That sounds like a patrol goose in trouble, Bob.

They paddled for the shore at top speed.

JUST AT THAT MOMENT, all the magic headphones went wrong. They weren't really magic, they were plastic and needed lots of batteries, which had run down.

Suddenly, all the animals could hear!

Noel Vole woke up first. He saw the
weasels jump on Godfrey's scooter. Then
Dick Duck, Betty Bantam, all the goslings,
the frog, even Godfrey the Gander
woke up. They all chased after the
weasels.

But the weasels had
reached the top of a
steep hill. They were
picking up speed.
It looked as if
they would get away.

Then – BRUMP? "CRUNCH The front wheel snapped clean off the scooter and rolled into the pond.

I've been meaning to mend that front wheel for weeks.

OW!

The weasels were thrown high into the air. They landed in a tangled and mangled whiskery heap.

They were half-way to Lucy's house when
the EEE-NONN note faltered and
crackled. Then it stopped altogether.
It was quiet. Too quiet.

Puffing and panting, they arrived at the goose house. The first thing they saw was Lucy. She was sitting in her bath, completely still. Her beak was wide open and there was a far-away look in her eyes. From inside the house came the faint, worn sound of a scratchy record.

Noel Vole rushed into the house and
moved the jammed needle . . .

"'CLICK''' Repeat after me, hey nonny no,
hey nonny no, hey nonny no.
When through the green fields they did pass,
In spring time, 𝄞
The only pretty ring time.
When birds do sing, ♪
Hey dinga linga ling, hey dinga linga ling.
Sweet lovers love the spring.

He quickly switched
it off.

I'm afraid she's lost her voice.
It's singing the same note for too
long that does it. It's happened
to friends of mine when they've
overcroaked. What she needs is
a holiday... **somewhere
quiet.**

Lucy's singing had saved the animals'
treasures from being stolen. They
forgot all about her keeping them awake.
In fact, they were so pleased with Lucy
that they used the reward money to send
her on a long holiday to the seaside.

Every morning, she gargled with salt
water and she spent every afternoon
eating ice-cream. In a few days her
voice had come back.

And of course,
just so she wouldn't be lonely, all the
other animals came with her.

They left the record-player at home.

Lucy's holiday at the seaside was nearly over. Her voice was back to normal and she could even hum, just a little. While the other animals were building a last big sand-castle on the beach, Lucy had wandered up the main street. She was looking for presents to take home.

She'd had a really good time on her holiday.
She'd tried every kind of ice-cream.

She'd been on the ghost train with Godfrey the Gander . . .

. . . three hundred and ninety-two times.

She'd been on the dodgems with Dick once.

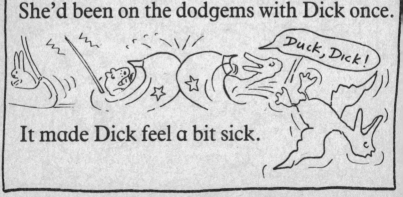

It made Dick feel a bit sick.

She'd had herself buried in sand . . .

. . . by experts.

She'd been waterskiing with Janet the Gannet.

And she'd got a really high score on the Whacka-Croc.

Well done! You have got a really high score on the Whacka-Croc.

WHACKA CROC

She had just come out of the sweet shop
when something made her stop and stare.

It was a fortune-teller's booth.
But it was no ordinary fortune-teller.
It was . . .

THE ORIGINAL ONE AND ONLY
MADAM KATIE
QUACKALENGRO

HORROR SCOPES
DOOM GLOOM
DESTRUCTION AND EARTHQUACKS A SPECIALITY

PALMIST TO THE STARS

strange flute music

Quacksess
GEEZA CARD
WELCOME

UNLOCK THE SECRETS OF KUPPA-TEA
PRICES TO SUIT ALL

UNTIE THE KNOT TO KNOWLEDGE. KNOW THE FUTURE NOW

What will the future hold for Lucy Goose?

Lucy shyly poked her head through the bead curtain. Pinned to a screen inside were lots of letters.

THE
WATER
HOLE
Nr. Lake
Victoria

Dear M.K.,
I did what
you said
and stuck
my neck
out. It
worked.
All the
best.
G. Raffe

DUCKINGTHEM PALACE

Dear Madam Katie,
    *Her Majesty has requested me
to thank you for your kind letter
congratulating the happy couple
and **predicting** a fine day for it.*
    Yours etc. 324

*LADY-IN-WAITING
No. 324*

No 102
Main St.
The Jungle

DEAR MADAM KATIE,
WELL SPOTTED!
Leopard

THE BUNGALOW
SAHARA DESERT
AFRICA

Dear Madam Katie,
    Thank you for your good advice.
Now I can see the funny side and we've
all had a good laugh about it!
    Regards, Tina Hyena
    -ha-ha
    TINA HYENA (Mrs)

From behind the screen came the
sound of strange flute music.
Lucy stepped carefully inside.
It seemed dark and gloomy after
the bright sunshine of the street.
It made her blink.
Then Lucy saw a
very large chair.
Sitting in it was
a very small duck.
On her head she
wore a bright
red scarf. It had
a pattern of
yellow horseshoes.
Around her neck
was a golden letter
K. It sparkled as
she spoke.

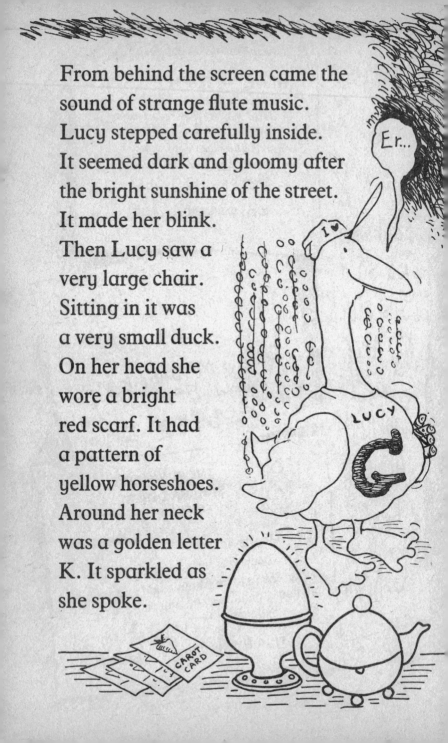

Come in my dear, don't be shy. I'm Madam Katie. Would you like the KUPPA-TEA LEAF SPECIAL, the FOOT READING or the CRYSTAL EGG GAZING? ARRH, QUACK! BUT WHAT FEET YOU HAVE! Quackly! Over here! It must be the FOOT READING. Put your left foot on this cushion. I'm beginning to feel a...

Suddenly Madam Katie began to sway slowly from side to side. Her bill wobbled and one of her toes began to twitch.

Lucy quickly sat down and put her foot on the cushion. Madam Katie stopped swaying. She bent forward and looked closely at the enormous orange foot. She began to speak again. . .

You will be **given a sign...** and it will get you off to **a flying start.**

But... oh dear... BEWARE! It's a bit blurred... I can't quite make it out... DANGER! PAIN! NO... YES... That's it! Watch out for large... big growing things? Dangerous— **Be careful of big vegetables!** I can see you **escorted along the promenade... dressed in white ribbons...** You are **On wheels...** in a great carriage, perhaps. **People step aside to let you pass.** You're **in the papers!** Everyone is talking about you...

oooooOh!

Madam Katie fell back in her chair. Her eyes were tight shut.

The fortune-telling was over. It was time for Lucy to foot the bill. She gave Madam Katie all her sticks of rock and a large ice-cream with chocolate in it. Then off she went, humming a happy little song.

Goodbye my dear... SLURP And bon chance. MUNCH

When I dropped into the fortune-teller, what a lucky day for me.

LUCY

Next door was an amusement arcade. Lucy remembered Madam Katie's words.

And your lucky number is... TWENTY TOE ... Sorry, twenty two.

I might win.

22

LUCKY FOR SOME

WHY DON'T YOU TRY?

She decided to try her luck. The shrew mouse, who had been waiting outside Madam Katie's booth, followed her inside.

Lucy walked out of the arcade with her nose in the air. She was very annoyed.

The tiny shrew mouse watched her leave. Then he crept over to the machine. He climbed up and tapped it gently.

WHIRRRRRRRRRR! The machine sprang into life. The letters spun round and lights flashed.

It began to shudder and shake. There was a loud CLANG! Out poured hundreds of coins. The machine began to play 'I Do Like To Be Beside The Seaside' very quickly.

But Lucy never heard a thing. She had walked down the road to the harbour. In front of her the road was closed. The sea wall was being repaired. A water rat in wellington boots was struggling with one end of a big sign. He shouted to Lucy:

Instantly, Madam Katie's words came back to her.

The water rat began directing a large
tractor across the road.

The tractor rolled right over her left foot.

Lucy dropped the sign with a shriek and flew high into the air.

Madam Katie's words flashed through her mind as she soared above the rooftops.

Off flew Lucy again, but now she was
heading straight for a large banner.

It got tangled round her neck. Down
below, in the Spa Ballroom, the finals of
the famous Go Prancing dance
championship were taking place.

Lucy and the
banner came
crashing through
the ballroom
roof.

Lucy landed on her injured foot SLAP,
BANG in the middle of the dance floor.
OOOH that hurt! She started to dance and
leap about in pain.

In a few minutes all the other dancers had been pushed over.

Bright and early the next morning, Godfrey the Gander collected Lucy from hospital. He took her for a walk along the sea front in her brand-new wheelchair. She remembered Madam Katie's last two predictions.

I can see you escorted along the promenade... dressed in white ribbons... You are on wheels... in a great carriage. People step aside to let you pass.

THROB

Hey! Careful!

1st PUSH-ME-OVA

You're in the papers!

Don't worry, Lucy. We're all staying another two weeks at the seaside and the bandages will be off by Christmas... with a bit of luck.

But Lucy was thinking about what the future might hold for a certain fortune-telling duck.

It was a bright moonlit night in early
September and the goslings were hard at
work making sandwiches.

Several hundred sandwiches later, they
had to stop. They'd run out of bread
and peanut butter. The sun was just
beginning to peep over the horizon.

'It's time we woke Lucy,' said Goslynn.

Lucy was sound asleep and had just reached a very interesting bit in one of her favourite dreams.

Lucy was still half asleep. She stuck her head out of the window and took a deep breath. Then she saw that it really was going to be a lovely day. The sun was already shining brightly and there wasn't a cloud in the sky. The horizon looked blue and inviting.

'Yes,' thought Lucy. 'It's just the kind of day for getting out. . .

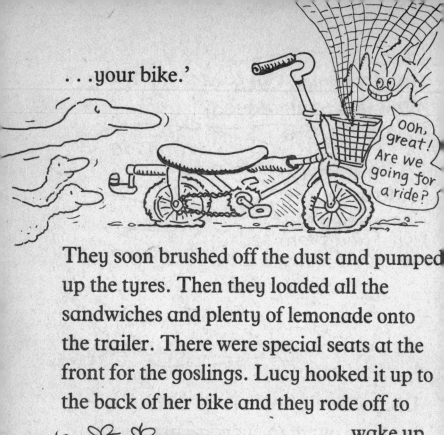

'. . .your bike.'

Ooh, great! Are we going for a ride?

They soon brushed off the dust and pumped up the tyres. Then they loaded all the sandwiches and plenty of lemonade onto the trailer. There were special seats at the front for the goslings. Lucy hooked it up to the back of her bike and they rode off to wake up the other animals.

Godfrey got out his scooter and Dick Duck
drove his bright-green pedal car. Noel
Vole's legs were too short for pedalling
but he was just the right size
to fit in the
basket on Lucy's
bike.

The goslings thought Dick's new car was wonderful.

That's a great car, Uncle Dick, but what's the thing with all the numbers on?—Those buttons and stuff?

That's my new car phone, children. It's really useful. **Watch this!**

He smiled at them proudly and dialled a number. He used his bill to press the buttons.
Then he spoke to it.

Now they were off. Out on the open road, heading for their favourite picnic place in the old wood.

Goz and Goslynn were very excited, but they sat quietly in their seats for at least five minutes. Then Goz saw a button in front of him. It looked very interesting.

'I wonder what it does,' he thought. 'If I just give it a little nudge. . .'

TOO LATE!

It was a tip-up trailer and that button
was the control. Now they were so high
up they had a good view of all the
branches growing over the road.

They stretched out their necks to try and grab the fruit as they passed, but it was just out of reach. Goz climbed out of his seat and Goslynn held on to his wing.

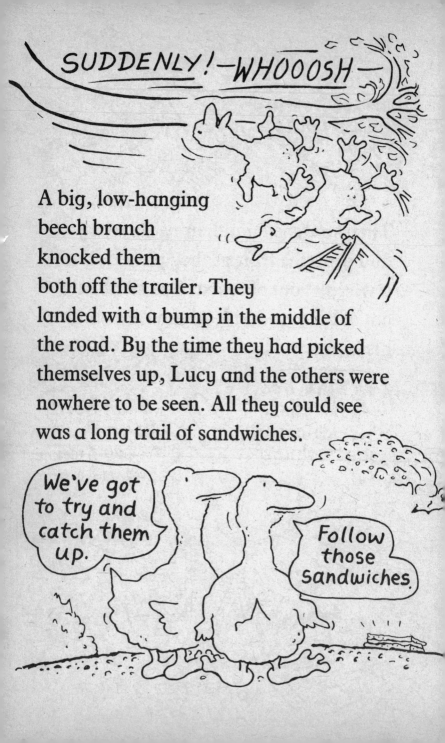

SUDDENLY! — WHOOOSH —

A big, low-hanging beech branch knocked them both off the trailer. They landed with a bump in the middle of the road. By the time they had picked themselves up, Lucy and the others were nowhere to be seen. All they could see was a long trail of sandwiches.

We've got to try and catch them up.

Follow those sandwiches.

Lucy, Godfrey, Dick and Noel didn't see the goslings fall out. They'd begun to free-wheel down the big hill at Swan Neck Bank. Lucy overtook Godfrey's scooter, but Dick was still out in front.

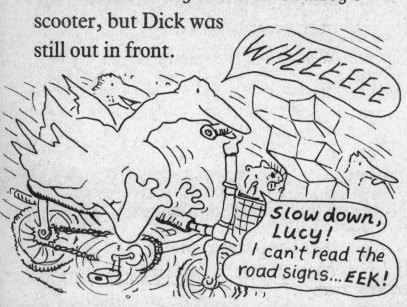

They rattled over a bridge, sped in and out of a dark tunnel, splashed across a couple of small streams and crunched their way through a thick hedge. They'd left the road miles behind and came to a stop in the middle of a ploughed field.

They were completely lost.

'That was great,' said Dick. 'But where are we?'

'Where are the sandwiches?' said Godfrey, looking at the empty trailer.

'Oh no! Where are the goslings?' said Lucy.

Noel was busy studying the map.

Can you see any landmarks? If I find them on the map, I'll know where we are.

An old mill, a church, that sort of thing.

'There's a five-barred gate over there,' said Lucy.

Sitting on the gate, watching them, was an old crow.

'Come on,' shouted Lucy. 'We've got to find those goslings.'

'And the sandwiches,' said Godfrey, as they set off back the way they had come.

They bumped over the ploughed field and fought their way through the little wood. They were carefully looking up at each tree trying to find the cuckoo's nest, when. . .

They'd fallen down an old mineshaft.

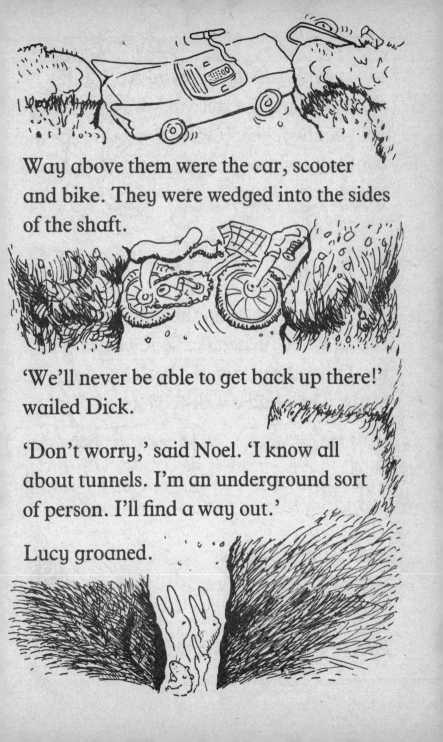

Way above them were the car, scooter
and bike. They were wedged into the sides
of the shaft.

'We'll never be able to get back up there!'
wailed Dick.

'Don't worry,' said Noel. 'I know all
about tunnels. I'm an underground sort
of person. I'll find a way out.'

Lucy groaned.

Meanwhile, on top of Swan Neck Bank, Goz and Goslynn were following the trail of spilt sandwiches. It was slow going, as they couldn't resist eating every one they found.

They were munching their way round a corner when, instead of sandwiches, the road ahead was covered with hundreds of birds. They had a well-fed look.

The goslings ran over to the phone box.

Goslynn climbed on Goz's back and began jumping up at the phone.

On the third go she knocked the hand piece out of its holder.

'What do we do now?' said Goz.
'You speak into it,' said Goslynn.

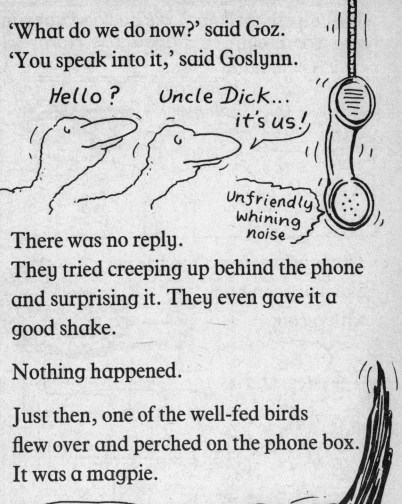

There was no reply.
They tried creeping up behind the phone
and surprising it. They even gave it a
good shake.

Nothing happened.

Just then, one of the well-fed birds
flew over and perched on the phone box.
It was a magpie.

The magpie flew off to her nest.
She was soon back
with a coin.

'Never mind,' said the magpie. 'It'll
be in the book. What's the name again?'
'Er...our uncle...Dick Duck...with
a D. It's his car phone,' said Goz.

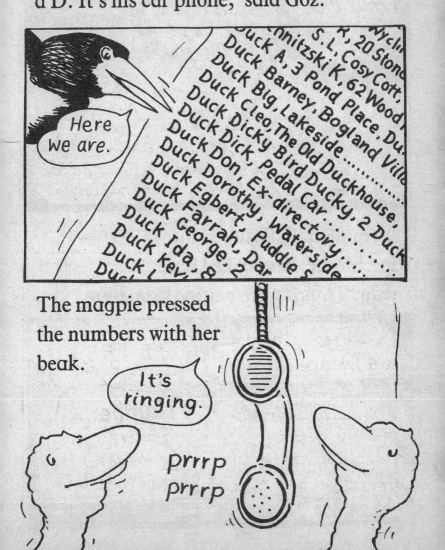

The magpie pressed
the numbers with her
beak.

Deep underground, Noel Vole was leading the way up a long tunnel.

A small moth fluttered into the torchlight. Noel asked it the way. Things were getting desperate.

> *Didn't you thee the thigns?*
> *THSTAY OUT. You thouldn't be here.*
> *You thould get out ath thoon ath*
> *pothsible.*

Godfrey lost his temper.

'We know that!' he shouted. 'You stupid moth!'

'Thorry, I'm thure,' said the moth. 'I might be thtupid, but I'M NOT LOTHT!'

And off he flew into the darkness.

Now the batteries in the torch were failing. Things were looking black. Even Noel, who was an underground sort of person, was getting worried.

Then they heard something. It was faint and far away, but it was definitely a . . .

. . . phone.

'It's my car phone!' yelled Dick. 'I'm sure it is.'

Brrp Prrp
Prrp

They clambered back through a maze of dark tunnels. The ringing was getting louder. Soon they were back at the place where they had fallen in. They looked up. Far above their heads, Dick's car phone was ringing. Perhaps someone would hear it and save them.

Then the ringing stopped.

It was deathly quiet.

'Oh dear,' thought Lucy.

Then a voice shouted down to them.
It was the old crow.

Anybody there called Duck?
Duck with a **D** ? Cawk
Somebody called Goslynn
wants a word with you.

YES!
ME! HELP!

'All right,' said the crow.
'Leave it with me.'
He spoke to the magpie on Dick's phone.
'That big goose, you know, the one who
gave away all those sandwiches, she's
stuck down the old mine.'
'Don't worry,' said the magpie. 'Leave
it with me.'
She phoned the garage.

... that's right...
Emergency... Rescue Service!

They sent a pick-up truck right away.
It picked up the goslings and dashed over
to the mine.

Soon Lucy, Godfrey, Dick and Noel had
all been safely hauled above ground.

'It's great to be out of there,' said
Godfrey with a shiver. 'But it's a shame
about the picnic.'

'It's OK,' said the crow. 'We've ordered you all take-aways on the car phone. They should be here any minute.'